Crog and Ally

For Oliver Bean—chaser of toys,
stealer of hearts, and the best
poodle friend I could ask for—DA

PENGUIN WORKSHOP
An imprint of Penguin Random House LLC, New York

First published simultaneously in paperback and hardcover in the United States of America by
Penguin Workshop, an imprint of Penguin Random House LLC, New York, 2022

Visit us online at penguinrandomhouse.com.

Library of Congress Cataloging-in-Publication Data is available.

Manufactured in China

ISBN 9780593387597 (hc)   10 9 8 7 6 5 4 3 2 1 TOPL

Designed by Julia Rosenfeld

Croc and Ally

A Lot to Like!

by Derek Anderson

Penguin Workshop

Ally Likes Blue

"I like blue.

Blue is the best color," said Ally.

"Croc, what color do you like?"

asked Ally.

"Red," said Croc.

"RED?" said Ally.

"How can you like red

when blue is the best?"

"I am making a blue circle,"
said Ally.

"Circles are the best shapes.

Croc, what shape do you like?"

"Squares," said Croc.

"*SQUARES?*" said Ally.

"How can you like squares

when circles are the best?"

"I am making seven pictures," said Ally.

"Seven is the best number.

Croc, what number do you like?"

"Nine," said Croc.

"*NINE?*" said Ally.

"How can you like nine

when seven is the best?"

"It is a good thing I like you so much," said Ally.

"You are one weird crocodile."

Pancakes!

"What do you want for lunch?"

asked Croc.

"Pancakes!" said Ally.

"Again?" said Croc.

"That is all you ever eat."

"Pancakes are my favorite food,"
said Ally.

"Come on.

We are going to find you

a new favorite food," said Croc.

Croc made some new foods

for Ally to try.

Ally liked toast with grape jelly.

Ally really liked grilled cheese

sandwiches with ketchup.

Ally really, really liked macaroni and cheese.

Ally really, really, really liked spaghetti and meatballs.

Ally was really, really, really full.
And Croc was really, really, really
tired of cooking.

"What is your favorite food *now*?"

asked Croc.

"Pancakes!" said Ally.

Little Croc

"What is that?" asked Croc.

"This is my new friend, Little Croc,"
said Ally.

"That is not your friend," said Croc.

"It is a smelly sock that looks like me."

"No," said Ally.

"Little Croc is not like you at all.

Watch this."

"Hey, Little Croc, are you grumpy?"
asked Ally.

"No, I'm *happy*," said Little Croc.

"Me too!" said Ally.

"Hey, Little Croc, what color do you like best?"

"Blue," said Little Croc.

"Me too!" said Ally.

"Hey, Little Croc, what do you like to eat?" asked Ally.

"Pancakes!" said Little Croc.

"Me too!" said Ally.

"This is not funny," said Croc.

"Little Croc, do *you* think this

is funny?" asked Ally.

"Yes," said Little Croc.

"Me too!" said Ally.

"Croc, I am only kidding," said Ally.

"You know I like you the best."

"Me too!" said Little Croc.